This is a book of poetry written by G
since she was a child. 'Laughs' covers
whereas the 'Life' poetry is a more se
hopes will resonate with her readers.
love and laughter and, of course, sadness too, but wouldn t
change a thing .

Gill has also written a book called 'Two by Two – A Lark on
an Ark,' which she insists is the result of an over-active
imagination, also available on Amazon

Gill is dedicating this book to her husband Bill, who features
in one or more of the poems in the hope he will forgive her!

Written by Gill Sayers

Contents:

I Wanted to go in the garden
Diet
Who first thought
Dust
I've exercised tonight
All creased and crumply
When you live with a man
When you are a giggler
No longer young
Time
I think I am losing my hair
Overhearing
I am going out today
My smalls
I wish I was pleasantly plump
Runners running amok!
I wish I didn't like food
Goldfish
Forty thousand feathers
Stairs

Children running
I am lucky
Little lady
Oh Tabitha
Small things
Life
It's so easy
I'd love to go out dancing
Happiness
Helping others
Yesteryear
Witch
Be careful what you wish for
Summer memories
I wish I could soar
Do fairies ride on blossom
Imagination
Birds flitting
Time passes
She sits there every day you know
There are times

A special dog
When
Come skip with me
I hear music
I thought I saw A fairy
Don't weep for me
Today
It is only
Treasure
There are times
I remember summers
Have you ever?
I'm finding it hard
Life can lead us
I was born in spring
Friends are like diamonds
What time we waste
Last night
These hands

I can see you still

I Wanted to Go in the Garden

I wanted to go in the garden

I thought that I'd do that today

I reached for my shoes and then got the news

Our grandsons are coming to play

I wanted to go in the garden

I'd taken some aspirin for pain

I'd put on my coat and was starting the gloat

When it suddenly started to rain

I wanted to go in the garden

I'd left the 'phone off the hook

I meant to go out, there wasn't a doubt

But I just had to finish my book

I wanted to go in the garden

Although I was feeling quite tired

I got all prepared, but then really despaired

When my energy had all expired

I wanted to go in the garden

There was only my husband and me

But we took a short rest, at my husband's request

And finally watched all the Grand Prix

I wanted to go in the garden

 I thought I had planned it OK

Then the telephone rang and my daughter's voice sang

Can you look after my daughter today?

Well, today I went in the garden

I dug and weeded with care

But, oh dear the pain, I won't do it again

Cos now I can't get out of my chair!

Diet

Monday – I started a diet

Feeling I am rather plump

So many clothes don't fit me

and I'm fed up with looking a frump

Breakfast was easy to cover

Cereals poured into a bowl

Strawberries added for flavour

I'd soon be reaching my goal

Midmorning found me challenged

No biscuits to dunk in my tea

I ate a banana, wasn't the same

But still feeling self- satisfied, me!

Come lunchtime I cooked myself pasta

Wasn't too bad I admit

But where was my cake, just an empty plate

Was feeling miserable without it

Skipped afternoon tea, we went out

This stopped my thinking of food

Felt quite a martyr did I

Couldn't believe I was being so good.

Dinner time came and I crumbled

We had fish and chips from the shop

Not the same without bread and butter

Filled myself up, I couldn't stop

Tuesday, I started a diet ....

Who First Thought

Who first thought of sausage rolls

Or batter mix for pancakes

Who knew cheese would go with ham

And tomatoes with pasta bakes

Who first thought about donuts?

Punch a hole and fill it with jam

To make bread and butter pudding

Or fritters being made with Spam

Who first decided on Liver with Bacon?

That big mushrooms would be better stuffed

Spaghetti would be that bit too long

Or make pastry that could be puffed.

Who had the thought that egg-whites

Whisked with sugar makes chewy meringues

Or that Welsh Rare it would be even tastier

With melting cheese that overhangs

Who decided peas should be mushy

Or peas could be frozen or canned

Frozen or Canned, Mushy or Dried

Some of them would be better banned

Why has honey been added to cornflakes

Or chocolate, so bad for your teeth

Why cover your meat with some pastry

When you can't see what's underneath

Decisions were made regarding to food

Too many choices I feel

Be you a meat eater or vegan

Can have something different every meal

Dust

Where does all the dust come from?

You can't see it in the air

It sneaks in under cover

Hiding here and there

Where does all the dirt come from?

It lurks on carpets with fluff

I hoover it up nearly every day

Get really fed up with the stuff

Where do all the weeds come from?

How do they grow through the drive?

I pull them all out when I find them

But more seem to come and then thrive

It's as though a war has been wagered

I'll never achieve squeaky clean

Think I'll pretend I can't see it

I'm sure you know just what I mean

I've Exercised Tonight

I've exercised tonight you know
I've swayed from left to right
I've waved my arms up in the air
And knew I looked a sight!

I've exercised tonight you know
And moved to an Abba song
I tried to pretend I liked it
But luckily it didn't last for long

I've exercised tonight you know
I laid down on a mat
I tried to look professional
But was no good at that

I've exercised tonight you know
We had to form a ring
We step- kicked towards each other
A bit like the Highland Fling

I've exercised tonight you know
We walked round and back again
We did the Shadows square walk thing
A strong core we need to attain

I've exercised tonight you know
We then had to wind down
We tried to look like we felt fit
Trying hard not to frown

I've exercised tonight you know

She thanked us all for attending

We really enjoyed it I heard others say

I wondered if they were pretending

I've exercised tonight you know

Not my 'thing' by half

And when I glanced at my friend's face

I found myself wanting to laugh

All Creased and Rumply

I feel all creased and rumply

What should be up hangs down

I can't see without my glasses

And I have a permanent frown

My arms flap when I move them

When still they hang around

My hands are fat but bony

And my eyelids can't be found

I have age spots on my age spots

And bruises everywhere

I knock into things so often

It really isn't fair

I ache in joints and muscles

And cannot stand too long

I can't remember when I last ran

It really is all wrong

If I fall over I can't get up

I make my family laugh

I know I look so funny

Because I don't do things by half

But, you know what, I am not sad

I do not feel the need

I've lived my life to the full

I'm the lucky one indeed

When You Live with a Man

When you live with a man who is clumsy

And has no control of his arms,

It's usually the things you treasure,

This caring, but clumsy man harms.

When he rushes to do things,

Because they must be done NOW

You tend to find yourself praying

That they'll stay undamaged somehow.

But when this man shows how he loves you

By trying to give you the moon

You realise you are so lucky,

And your clumsy man is a boon.

Or so I tell myself daily,

As another new mug hits the floor

But these are only possessions

And leave me room to get more.

Those arms have often held me

While I grieved for Mum and Dad

Or even when I'm hurting or

Generally feeling quite sad.

He's such a joy to live with,

He always makes me laugh

And when he does things for me,

He doesn't do them by half

So, replacing this loving man

Would not be possible to do

And I'll live with his little problem,

Because I've got some drawbacks too

We all have little accidents

I often trip and fall

He patiently helps me to get up

And doesn't laugh at all!

(Poetic licence used in the last line, of course he laughs,

but only after ensuring I am ok!)

When you are a Giggler

This is a poem wot I wrote while I was sitting thinking

It sort of popped into my head, and, no, I've not been drinking!

When you are a giggler, it only takes one word

For you to fall to pieces because of what you've heard.

When you are a giggler, it only takes a look

For mirth to overwhelm you, despite the breath you took.

When you are a giggler and something makes you laugh

You have to hold your tummy, while you're nearly bent in half

When you are a giggler, and tears rolling down your cheeks

You have to cross your legs you know, in case of other 'leaks!'

When you are a giggler, with friends who are the same

You feed off one another and you are so glad that they came

When you are a giggler, life is so much fun

Memories are happy with the giggling you have done

So come on all you gigglers, go out and spread the news

A good laugh can work miracles and blow away the blues!

No Longer Young

My hair was always curly

No drier for me don't you know

Sometimes it can look quite unruly

But sod it, I just wash and go

My face is fatter and wrinkly

And I think my nose has grown bigger

My eyelids have gone all droopy

And my lips are thinner - go figure

When it comes to my hands they're misshapen

It hasn't always been so

But arthritis has finally got me

Oh how I wish it would go!

And as for my body - it's lost it

Dips and droops where it will

I have grown twice my size since I married

And I'm blaming all that on Bill

My legs aren't doing too badly

My ankles aren't swollen like some

But the tops are luckily hidden

Especially where they join my bum

Now my feet have always been bony
With curling toes that should not
Some now look like they have quarrelled
Yep, my feet don't look all that hot!

I'll admit my brain has got slower
Sometimes words will not come to mind
 I have to describe what I'm meaning
Old age really is not kind!

Although I'm no longer youthful
I'm happier with me as I am
I've learned what is most important
For the rest .... I don't give a damn!

Time

Time is moving swiftly on

Hours just rush on by

I have so much I need to do

It really makes me sigh

I try to get up earlier

Make the day stretch out

But that does not work either

What's that all about?

Thought of writing out a list

And crossing off what's done

But the list would really put me off

And that would be no fun

So, I've made a decision

Some things will have to slip

That'll be the boring stuff

Leaving me time for a kip

I Think I am Losing My Hair

I think I am losing my hair

The thickness is no longer there

It must be a sign of old age

The turning of another new page

My back hurts, knees not up to par

I really can't walk very far

Guess I'll soon be using a stick

Which will really get on my wick.

I'm shrinking in size, what a pain

Can't reach things up high, it's insane

I have to climb on a stool

Carefully, cos I am the fool

Who trips over nothing, just falls

With a talent for knocking against walls

Walking into open doors

Also well acquainted with floors

Old age is a pain in the arse

We're taught nothing about it in class

There is one aspect that's fine

I get away with not towing the line!

Overhearing

When you are minding your own business while waiting for a bus
And two people walk by saying, "Listen, just between us!"
You find yourself tuning in to what they're going to say
It just begins to get interesting, but then they walk away.

When you're in a waiting room, and hear somebody say,
"It stuck in a bottle, just the other day!"
Your mind starts working overtime, wondering what got stuck
A doctor then calls them in and you think, 'That's just my luck.'

And then there is another thing that makes you want to spit
You hear the most interesting line, 'And that's why she crushed it'
The damn frustration of wondering who, or what or why
You want to stop and ask them, but you can only sigh.

But worst of all is the teenage girl, who is talking on her phone
Always very loudly, her conversation makes you groan
As she spills the details, of what he said six times
You wonder if phone-icide is among hanging crimes

I Am Going Out Today

I am going out today and really looking fat

So I put on 'tummy holder ins' thinking that is that

But now the fat's above my waist hanging over my belly

It wibble wobbles looking odd, a bit like wearing jelly.

I took the 'holder ins' back off sighing with relief

Stop worrying I told myself I can hide it underneath

A top that doesn't hug me tight of which I have a few

When I choose the right one I know that it will do

So here I sit, in all my glory, elasticated waisted

Loose top hanging past my hips and feeling quite elated!

My Smalls

I hung my smalls upon the line

Despite the lack of warm sunshine

But there they hung all limp and wet

Not one bit of wind did they get!

Oh bugger, I thought, what a shame

When suddenly Bill called out my name

Be grateful he said that it is calm

Cos your big pants won't come to harm

Filled with air, they'd take off for sure

And your pants would be no more

I counted to ten, no, make that twice

Thinking now that wasn't nice

So being me, I am plotting revenge

Cos this is something I need to avenge!

I Wish I was Pleasantly Plump

I wish I was pleasantly plump

And not quite so big in the rump

I'd love to be lithe and more fit

Instead of sagging a bit

With a few less lines on my face

And eyelids that stayed in their place

Even my lips are too thin

Seems aging is really a sin

But, now I am thinking this through

Why are these making me blue?

I've made the most of my life

As friend, mother and wife

Let's face it, this is me

Who I am – who else would I be?

I have so much more to achieve

And I'm going to enjoy it, believe!

Runners Running Amok!

It's time to grow some beans again
I put three in every pot
I watered them all daily
And what a lot I got!

I began to feel excited
As I built a runner frame
Then planted the beans accordingly
Two per pole the same

These beans I nurtured carefully
Round poles I watch them twine
I check out those around me
None are as good as mine!

The flowers start to burst out
I've grown two different sorts
I can feel elation building
It's like being into sports!

The race is still progressing
As I pick the first long beans
I leave them casually on display
'I'm the winner!' is what this means

And so it goes on daily

We pick and pick and pick

We give them to our neighbours

Of beans we are quite sick!

We give them to our postman

We give them to our friends

We give them to acquaintances

The giving never ends

Out goes Bill with a bag of beans

To knock on every door

But everyone pretends they're out

They can't take it anymore!

The moral of this story is

Remember this next year

And only plant the minimum

But it will happen again I fear

I Wish I Didn't Like Food

I wish I didn't like food,

I find it so hard to say no

Roast potatoes and chips

Why do I enjoy them so?

Cake that is filled with fresh cream,

Chocolate that melts in my mouth

Cashews roasted with salt

Are making my tummy go south

I have trouble wearing my clothes

Now some no longer fit

I look in the mirror and I'm aghast

Am I slender, not even a bit

I say I will go on a diet

And then I start eating more junk

Tea? Yes I would love one please,

With a biscuit or two I can dunk!

Goldfish

Once we had a goldfish

Won it at a fair

It lived upon the windowsill

Loved to see it there

We went away on holiday

Left Bill's dad in charge

When we can home, it wasn't there

Had it grown too large?

Went into the garden

Found a cross of lolly sticks

 Fish was underneath it

Poor Dad was pooping bricks

Seems he overfed it

Came in and found it dead

Gave it a lovely funeral

Well, that is what he said

We'd had that fish for several years

Did feel rather sad

But looking back on it now

Really can't blame Bill's dear dad!

Forty Thousand Feathers

Forty thousand feathers on a thrush's throat

Who's the idiot who counted them?

And did he rock the boat?

Why are owls considered wise?

And who called candles 'candles?'

Who penned the name 'Flash Mobs?'

Why so many handles?

Not seen anyone 'lifting spirits'

Or someone too big for his boots

How can you 'get down - on it?'

Or go looking for your roots?

Why is the sky your limit?

Who put breadcrumbs onto ham?

Why am I asking these questions?

When I know you don't give a damn!

Stairs

Stairs seem like a mountain Going up or going down

They're not too bad with handrails

But they always make me frown

I get a sense of achievement

When I make it to the top

But I hate the ones with high steps

Cos my knees begin to pop

I should stop wearing long skirts

As I have to hold them high

Clutching my bag in the same hand

Every time I wonder why

I have been known to tumble

From the top down to below

Luckily it was in a store

Though my 'smalls' were there on show

Stairs seem like a mountain

I feel I need a rope

And a pair or two of crampons

They'll make it easier to cope

Thoughts on Life

Children Running

Children Running, pitter patter

Running forward, hear them chatter

Laughter bubbling from inside

Excited eyes open wide

Arms outstretched to welcome life

They know nothing yet of strife

They know nothing yet of sorrow

Of worrying about tomorrow

Days for them are full of joy

Full of play, that special toy

Of Mother's love and Father's pride

That he's the one to be their guide

Children running, pitter patter

Today what does the future matter?

I am Lucky

I realise I am lucky surrounded by love and care
There are so many people who have nobody there

I realise I am lucky I really can't complain
I don't suffer like some others who are struggling with pain

I realise I am lucky I believe my loved ones crossed
Visit with me constantly so I don't feel so lost

I realise I am lucky I have this firm belief
That I will see them all again which lessens any grief

Little Lady

Little old lady, old and frail

Ample rouge to hide the pale

Face all wrinkled, hair now grey

Living out each weary day

But deep inside there burns a joy

Of memories, that special boy

Their happiness of being together

Of passing storms they had to weather

Little old lady, see her smile

She was young again just for a while.

Oh Tabitha

Oh Tabitha!

You naughty girl

Just look what you have done

You've set the birdcage in a whirl

The cat is on the run.

You climbed upon the table

Then left some scratches there

Why can't you be more stable

Beneath that golden hair.

You scratch the door, and empty bins

You steal our precious treasures

We chastise you, but we never win

No matter what the measures

Last week you even ate a pound –

Oh, who would have an Afghan Hound?

Small Things

Sometimes it's just the small things

That bring us so much pleasure

 Like walking around a favourite shop

Admiring things at leisure

Sometimes it's just a simple word

Can lift your spirits high

Being told you're looking well

As a friend goes walking by

Sometimes just a little touch

On your hand or on your arm

Makes you feel so cherished

Acting like a charm

Sometimes being hugged close

Can make you feel so good

Especially when it isn't rushed

Taking longer than it could

But, there's another thing you know

That sets my heart a-quiver

It's when I'm made a cup of tea

And I'm a taker, not a giver!

Life

Life is too short to worry

This just causes more

Life is too short for anger

Need to show that the door

Life is too short for 'If onlys'

And the regrets they always bring

Life is too short for wishes

'I wish I'd not done 'that' thing

Life is too short for saying

Something you'd later regret

Life is too short for ignoring

The problems your loved ones can get

But life's not too short for laughter

All the joy that bubbles inside

And life's not too short for loving

As our capacity for this is so wide

It's So Easy

It's so easy to make mistakes

And decisions that are wrong

Life doesn't come with guarantees

For perfection we all long

We can only do our best

There is no other way

Most times it can turn out right

We can keep bad things at bay

But once in a while, no matter what

We are blinded to reality

We walk in with eyes open wide

Losing the truth of what we see

However, this can be redeemed

If we are determined enough

We can always right the wrong

Although it can be tough

I'd Love to go out Dancing

I'd love to go out dancing
To kick up my heels and twirl
I'd love spin round like a top
'til my head is all awhirl.
To move in time to music
Feel the beat up through my feet
Dance like no one's watching
That would be so neat
To sway to music slowly
In the arms of someone dear
To wrap my arms around him
To hold my loved one near

Happiness

Even though life can be hard, happiness should be sought

What cheers me up I ask myself (Doing things I didn't ought!)

Opening curtains, seeing the sun, feeling warmth through the window pane

Or even when the rain pours down knowing the garden will gain

Watching the birds building their nests, gathering bits and pieces

Flying here and flying there their work pace never ceases

When elderly neighbours stand and chat and I can hear their laughter

No loneliness there I tell myself as they head indoors right after

Young children who are running by told to take care by Mum

They don't hear as they're busy enjoying time with their chum

Dogs that are resting after their walk and you know they're feeling safe

They trust us to make sure they have nothing bad to face.

When looking at a partner, child or friend and feel my heart expand

With the love within for them and knowing they understand

Happiness too in feeling the strength of knowing this is me

And not letting others undermine who I really want to be

Happiness takes so many forms, I've listed but a few

There's crispy roast potatoes and delicious pastries too

Not forgetting music, that seems to cleanse my soul

To always look for happiness, is my lifelong goal

Helping Others

Happiness can be catching this is something I have found

But then again, so's sadness which also can abound

I know that I am lucky now life is really good

I've had struggles too, wouldn't change them if I could

My Father always told me you'll learn something every day

He was right you know, bless him, it really seems that way

Today I learned that love expands, there is more and more to share

And how important it can be to make sure I am there

For someone who is hurting as their eyes fill up with tears

Asking for protection to help them through their fears

It truly is an honour to help lift up their hearts

To rub their backs, or hold their hands until the healing starts

I have reached my twilight years and have learned so much

People always feel better with a loving touch

We need to help each other as we can't exist alone

A little hug, a word or two a gossip on the phone.

Speak to that lovely lady who is struggling to walk by

Leaning on her walking stick issuing a sigh

Smile at those who catch your eye it will make them feel much better

Most of us use Internet but some would love a letter

Listen when they answer so they know you really care

Spare sometime to walk with them it doesn't matter where

We need to help each other we can't exist alone

Some peoples' days are empty because they're on their own

Yesteryear

Us elders are shocked by the prices

They're so costly for what you get

We can't help compare with the old days

When our fear was having a debt

Takeaways were much more simple

We just had fish and chips

And if we could, pickled onions

And vinegar that burned our lips

But now food all seems 'designer'

With wraps and strange foreign bread

Meals served with odd sounding sauces

Not with lettuce, but 'salad leaves' instead

We yearn for plain rolls and butter

Just like they all used to be

Instead we have Ciabatta, Rye bread

Or something called Panini

And we have trouble with mobiles

They seem to do far too much

We're frightened of all those damn symbols

As we know there are some not to touch

But, we do understand home cooking

And how to add in our heads

We were also taught to heal arguments

At night before we went to bed

However, I feel we were lucky

Our lives were more modest by far

We played in the street as children

And we were rarely disturbed by a car

Although it seems now is better

Press a button and things will appear

I can't help feel we're all searching

For the simplicity of yesteryear!

Witch

I've often been called a witch

though it's never made me rich

It's because I just seem to know

who is friend and who is foe

I can tell if they're full of hot air

or if they really are aware

It has stood me in good stead

to know what goes on in their head

So, I would rather be labelled this way

and have true friends any day

Be Careful What You Wish For

Be careful what you wish for I've often heard it said

I try to think so carefully, thoughts running through my head

I think, 'I'll wish for messages that come from loved ones passed.'

But this can't always happen, and that thought doesn't last.

I wish hard for a fortune, enough money to go around,

It would seem as though I have enough, no pot of gold is found!

Perhaps I'll wish for glory, where everyone knows me

But that wish can't be granted, I am ordinary, see?

One day perhaps I'll write that book, it will be a certain hit

This wish is near impossible, but I try to, bit by bit.

When young I wished so many things, while sitting up a tree

To be a ballet dancer or catch a fairy I longed to see.

I've given wishing lots of thought, I know we all can try

But wishing can be selfish, I'm sure you all know why.

So, instead, I wish YOU happiness, perhaps one from the list above,

And I wish you joy in little things, but I mostly wish you ... love!

Summer Memories

The summer brings such memories of a childhood filled with fun

The days all seemed much longer as we played out in the sun

The summer brings such memories of paddling in the stream

And climbing trees up to the top much higher than they seem

The summer brings such memories of cycling with your friends

And chatting to each other while careering round the bends

The summer brings such memories off out with Mum and Dad

Taking a trip to the seaside and the ice cream we all had

The summer brings such memories of children of your own

Keeping up traditions because it's all that you have known

The summer brings such memories of family now passed

Who made you who you are today, the time has gone so fast

The summer brings such memories the ones we've made together

The special things we've said and done no matter what the weather.

The summer brings such memories making the most of every day

Spending time with friends and family so they are able to say .....

'The summer brings such happiness'

I Wish I Could Soar

I wish I could soar like a bird as I watch them cruise overhead

But not for me the birds eye view I am tied to the ground instead

I imagine how it would feel to float above trees and fields

Riding thermals so effortlessly while the height so gradually builds

I wish that I could sing like a bird as I land on the branch of a tree

To tell my story in song and how wonderful it feels to be free

But then I am reminded how I can sit and clear my mind

Then imagine am flying leaving the earth behind!

Do Fairies Ride on Blossom

Do fairies ride on blossom that floats down from the tree?

Do they pick up the bird feathers, at least the ones they see?

Do they dance at night in circles underneath the moon

And wear out their tiny slippers as morning comes too soon?

Do they have the choice of flowers they tend with loving care

Do they have a special one, or do they often share?

And does that rustle we can hear from down among the flowers,

Mean they're busy working, which they probably do for hours?

Do they ring their tiny bells to show when they are done,

And gather all together as it's time to have some fun?

So let's sit still and listen, we may hear their fairy cries

And suddenly catch sight of them from the corners of our eyes!

Imagination

Imagination is a wonderful thing, picturing dreams and wishes

 I often let my mind wander away when I am doing the dishes

I go on autopilot, while gazing at the sky

Then I go inside into myself as thoughts are filtered by

I see myself upon a hill, scanning distant views

Watching cars and people, fields of different hues

I can hear the birdsong rising, floating through the air

Whistling combined with chirping, wonder what they share

To my left are cowslips, mingling with the clover

To my right hawthorn trees, but they are further over

A gentle breeze ruffles my hair, although not very much

Reminding me of something ,oh yes, a loved one's touch

Suddenly the doorbell rings, the dogs begin to clamour

Back to the present I am drawn, to the opposite of glamour

But, do you know, I feel refreshed, my heart is feeling light

I feel so calm amid the noise, in fact, I feel 'just right!'

Birds Flitting

To see birds flit from tree to tree

Seems to calm my heart

To hear them chirping and whistling their songs

Gives mornings a magical start

They always seem so busy

Collecting items for their nest.

It's as though they're on a mission,

Mornings, it seems are best.

I wish they knew the joy they are

To watch with human eyes

To see them busily fly around

Lifts my spirit to the skies

Please take time from your busy days

To listen while they sing

Just five minutes is all you need

For the peacefulness they bring

Time Passes

Time passes by year by year and children leave the nest

Memories now mean oh so much, though they are second best

Take the time to share your thoughts with those who fill your heart

Please don't wish you'd done so when it's their time to depart

Share your love, say it out loud, and hug them close to you

It's these things they'll remember when your time on earth is through

Tomorrow comes much faster now, believe me, this is so

Tell your loved ones how you feel, time to let them know.

She sits there every day You Know

She sits there every day you know, peering at the sky

Every now and then she nods, those passing wonder why

She sits there every day you know, she's often heard to sigh

While other times she shakes her head and then begins to cry

She sits there every day you know, all alone and sad

With memories of a loved one and the happiness they had

She sits there every day you know from morning until dark

When she'll gather her belongings and slowly leave the park

She sits there every day you know until one day she's not

People see the empty seat and gather in a knot

She sits there every day you know they mutter one and all

As they realise they miss her and heard she took a fall

She sat there every day you know just waiting for the day

She could join her husband as she gladly passed away

There are Times

There are times we seem to struggle, and feel so very low

There seems no reason for it, or not one that we know

We ought to make the effort to do what must be done

And when we get around to it, it doesn't seem much fun

Let's all band together, and let us make a pact

To try to be more upbeat, and less more matter of fact

Bring in positive thinking, look for good and not bad

Make the effort to be happy, find a reason to be glad!

A Special Dog

We said goodbye, it broke our hearts

Though we knew the time had come

I hugged him close, he seemed to know

His look said, 'Goodbye Mum.'

I see him now, out with his Dad

The joy on both their faces

Man and his dog, that special bond

That nothing else replaces

It's over now, his pain has gone

He's running free above

It will take time to mourn his loss

But we'll remember him with love.

When

When raindrops hit the water and I'm all cosy and warm

When thunder rolls around the hills in the middle of a storm

When sun shines through the window and bounces off the glass

When snow drifts down so quietly and gently carpets' grass

When hail drops suddenly from the sky and bounces on the ground

When clouds are skidding way up high, making not a sound

When wind is blowing strongly bending tops of trees

When it turns into gale force, knocking us to our knees

When every day is different, and our wardrobes overlap

When our Country's weather changes in each part of the map

That's when I feel so grateful to be living as I do

Because life is full of changes, it's like the weather too!

Come Skip With Me

Come skip with me, let's act all silly

Let's giggle and laugh out loud

Come sing with me, we'll make up the words

And stand out from the crowd

Come dance with me, we can twirl around

And stomp along with the beat

Come dine with me, we'll sit together

In companionship while we eat

Come walk with me, and take my arm

And tell me all your sorrows

Come sit with me, and hold my hand

And we'll plan our tomorrows

Come visit me when you have passed

And I'm wishing you were here

Come dream with me when I'm asleep

And whisper in my ear

Come give me strength to carry on

And get up every day

Come meet me when my time is near

To take me on my way

I hear the Music

I hear the music and I want to dance

Which I will do given half a chance

I feel my feet begin to tap

While my hands would like to clap!

Before I know it, I'm on my feet

Moving to the music's beat

Not too fast, I might fall over

Slow to middling and I'm in clover

There'll be a cost, I know that's true

There's a limit to what my body can do

Tomorrow I will pay the price

Because moving to music feels so nice!

I Thought I Saw a Fairy

I thought I saw a fairy

 Dancing through the flowers

She had a leaf umbrella

Because of April showers

I heard her tinkling laughter

When she ducked out of our view

Sit quietly in your garden

And you might see one too!

Don't Weep For Me

Don't weep for me, I'm happy here and out of all my pain.

Heaven is so beautiful, and we will meet again.

I am forever grateful that you chose me as your pet

An oh so loving owner, the best a dog could get

Please promise me, that though you grieve

It will be for just a while

And when you feel me visit you, you'll greet me with a smile.

I had to go, it was my time to meet up with my 'Mum'

And I will visit often through the days and years to come

Today

Today I heard some music which made me think of Mum,

Of laying on the floor with her as visions started to come.

The music touching both our hearts we did not say a word,

Engrossed in what we were 'seeing' from the melody we heard.

I felt the tears start welling up at this childhood memory

Until I realised the truth, Mum was sending it to me!

It is Only

It is only a little blue flower

It doesn't show off at all

But it has an important message

That we should all recall

It shares a loving reminder

To us who grieve a lot

We must carry on living

Though they ask, 'Forget-me-not'

Treasure!

Treasure the people you love

Treasure the peace you can find

Treasure the laughter you hear

Treasure the thoughts in your mind

Treasure the memories shared

Treasure the gifts you've received

Treasure the songs you have heard

Treasure the truth you believed

Treasure the way your heart beats

Treasure the way you can see

Treasure the loving words that are said

Treasure what you mean to me

There are Times

There are times in life you know when memories flood in

One leads to another, some can make you grin

There are times in life you know when you think you hear a voice

Belonging to someone that you miss, you wish you had that choice

There are times in life you know when a smell comes wafting by

Reminding you of a loved one passed, all you can do is sigh

There are times in life you know when someone calls your name

You turn but there is no one there but you heard it just the same

There are times in life you know when you wish with all you might

That they are with you one more time if only for one night

I Remember Summers

I remember summers that lasted forever

The sun just shone every day

We could wake up early and play outside

It seemed like that anyway

There were trees to be climbed, flowers to be picked

Picnics to eat in the park

Calling for friends, riding our bikes

Staying out until it got dark

We'd paddle barefooted in the pond

Dirt squelching through our toes

Trying to catch sticklebacks using nets

Hiding in long grass in the meadows

And if the fair came to the common

We would queue for the candy floss

Then try to win a goldfish

Using hoops we had to toss

I remember summers that lasted forever

It was wonderful being a child

We all turned brown as berries...........

And reading this through, I smiled!

Have you Ever?

Have you ever considered Time?

 It can go fast or very slow

Morning hours can rush on by

Afternoons can take hours to go

When you're young the days seem long

But as you age, they're shorter

Where you used to rush around

Time now gives you no quarter

Things that used to take five minutes

Now take half an hour

And it seems to take much longer

To get into the shower

When you're waiting for your holiday

The days seem twice as long

But when you're there the time just flies

That really is so wrong

Have you ever considered time?

Waste it, we should not

Before you know it, it's all gone

So make the most of what you've got!

I'm finding it hard

I'm finding it hard to live on my own

Everything seems so strange

I used to be able to talk things through

I wasn't prepared for the change

However, I need to get stronger

I know I can go it alone

I am a woman, and women survive

Because we have a strong backbone

I admit I am feeling quite lonely

I admit I fear what's to come

But I am taking control of my future

To doubt I will never succumb

You wait, give me time and I'll show you

A totally different me

I'll be proud of all my achievements

From 'if onlys' I will be free!

Life Can Lead Us

Life can lead us on a merry dance

Bring us down given half a chance

Make us wish for other things

Instead of those our life brings

We must remember, to ourselves be true

Too much for others we can do

We give and give, don't seem to take

Which is such a big mistake.

Time to listen to our voices

Time to make some different choices

Loving ourselves is what we need

Not giving in to others greed

They will simply suck us dry

Then when they're done, just walk on by

Don't let life lead us astray

Consider our own lives, may I say

I was Born in Spring

I was born into my Spring oh so small and tight

Gradually I opened and reached out for the light

I gained my full potential getting stronger through the days

I spread myself out to the full in all the usual ways

My Summer came, I was full grown and thought my strength would hold

I enjoyed the 'heat' of longer days which made me rather bold

Then I reached my Autumn year, I felt the winds so strong

But I still had juice left in me and held on for so long

I clung to life as best I could when my Winter came so fast

Looking rather withered, a relic of the past

Others died around me while I held to my belief

My end came with a sudden gust, which dislodged this old brown leaf

I lay there with the others, around our Mother's roots

And eventually got trampled under children's boots

But, worry not, I will return, you've not seen the last of me

Next Spring I'll be found hanging upon the re-awakened tree

Friends are Like Diamonds

Friends are like diamonds if they remain true

And stand there beside you whatever you do

Friends are like blankets wrapped round yourself

Whenever you're lonely or not in good health

Friends are like raindrops that fall when you need

To be nourished and supported and helped to succeed

Friends are like sunshine they warm up your heart

And lift your spirits when sadness can start

Friends share your laughter, friends give support

Friends give you comfort, these things can't be bought!

Friends will forgive you when you just sit staring

Just being there, beside you, showing their caring

What Time we Waste

What time we waste in moaning because perfection is not ours

When we should all be rejoicing at the beauty of the flowers

The majesty of trees so tall reaching for the sky

The magic sound of water as it gently flows on by

Bird songs, all so different like music in the air

The gentle whisper of the wind as it ruffles through our hair

The clouds on high like cotton wool which change shape at a glance

Raindrops falling on the earth in a strange sort of dance

Sunsets and Sunrises that set the sky aglow

Autumn leaves to 'shush' through before it starts to snow

These things don't cost a penny we get them all for free

But what is so important is we take the time to see

Last Night

Last night I slept like a log

I'm feeling full of steam

It doesn't happen that often

And I didn't even dream

I usually lie and watch the clock

Ticking away the hours

Sleeping seems a waste of time

Wish I had super powers.

Just think about what I could do

With eight more hours to spare

There'd be no interruptions

I'd have more time to share

Ah, wait a minute, I've just thought

Of all the things I'd miss

A bit of time just to relax

That is always bliss

I'm not going to change my hours

It would be such a mistake

I'll make the most of what sleep I get

As rests I can always take

These Hands

These hands have buttoned up my clothes

And helped to dress another

These hands have shaken other hands

And held the hands of Mother

These hands have sewn and knitted too

And caressed my children's faces

These hands have taught them how to play

And tie up their shoe laces

These hands have held a husband near

And offered him support

They've prepared a multitude of food

While I've been lost in thought

These hands have hugged so many friends

And wiped away some tears

They've written many poems

And stroked away some fears

These hands have served me very well

And always done their best

 I guess I wanted all to know

That with these hands I'm blessed

An excerpt from my Spiritual Poems

I Can See You Still

I can see you still you know
I'm really not that far
I want you to imagine
I am sitting on a star
I hear you calling out my name
You always sound distraught
I put my arms around you
But you are grieving as you ought
One day when you are ready
I'll visit in your dreams
I will seem so real to you
As the light around me beams
So know I'm here, feel me close
Call me when you need
I'll wrap my love around you
As loved you are indeed

41917461R00042

Printed in Poland
by Amazon Fulfillment
Poland Sp. z o.o., Wrocław